Hamster Holmes

A MYSTERY COMES KNOCKING

By **Albin Sadar**

Illustrated by **Valerio Fabbretti**

Ready-to-Read

Simon Spotlight

New York   London   Toronto   Sydney   New Delhi

To my *great* nieces and
my *great* nephews! — A. S.

An imprint of Simon & Schuster Children's Publishing Division
1230 Avenue of the Americas, New York, New York 10020
First Simon Spotlight edition May 2015
Text copyright © 2015 by Albin Sadar
Illustrations copyright © 2015 by Valerio Fabbretti
SIMON SPOTLIGHT, READY-TO-READ, and colophon are registered trademarks
of Simon & Schuster, Inc.
For information about special discounts for bulk purchases, please contact Simon & Schuster
Special Sales at 1-866-506-1949 or business@simonandschuster.com.
Manufactured in the United States of America 0415 LAK
10 9 8 7 6 5 4 3 2 1
Library of Congress Cataloging-in-Publication Data
Sadar, Albin.
Hamster Holmes, a mystery comes knocking / by Albin Sadar ; illustrated by Valerio Fabbretti.
pages cm. — (Hamster Holmes ; 1) (Ready-to-read. Level 2)
Summary: "Hamster Holmes solves mysteries with his sidekick, a firefly named Dr. Watt! Corny
O'Squirrel is having trouble sleeping because someone keeps knocking on his door late at night.
Can they find out who is knocking, and why?"— Provided by publisher.
ISBN 978-1-4814-2036-5 (paperback) — ISBN 978-1-4814-2037-2 (hc) — ISBN 978-1-4814-2038-9
(ebook)
[1. Mystery and detective stories. 2. Detectives—Fiction. 3. Hamsters—Fiction. 4. Animals—
Fiction.]
I. Fabbretti, Valerio, illustrator. II. Title. III. Title: Mystery comes knocking.
PZ7.1.S23Ham 2015
[E]—dc23
2014048492

Hamster Holmes was a
very smart detective.
He solved mysteries
by thinking really, really hard.
"I've got it!" he said
as a light flashed over his head.
But it wasn't a lightbulb.
It was his friend,
a firefly named Dr. Watt.

Dr. Watt used Morse code
to get his point across.
He blinked his light on and off
to form the dashes and dots.
A long flash of light was a dash.
A short flash of light was a dot.

A •-
B -•••
C -•-•
D -••
E •
F ••-•
G --•
H ••••
I ••

J •---
K -•-
L •-••
M --
N -•
O ---
P •--•
Q --•-
R •-•

S •••
T -
U ••-
V •••-
W •--
X -••-
Y -•--
Z --••

"Dot-dot-dot-dot, dot-dot,"
flashed Dr. Watt.
Hamster Holmes thought
really hard.
"Four dots stand for the letter *H*.
Two dots stand for the letter *I*.
It spells 'hi'!" Then he waved.
"Why, hi to you too, Dr. Watt!"

Just then they heard the doorbell.
It was their friend
Corny O'Squirrel.
"Come in!" Hamster Holmes said.

"I am sorry to bother you,"
Corny replied with a yawn,
"but I need your help to solve
a mystery!"
"That's what we're here for,"
said Hamster Holmes.

"Someone keeps knocking
on my door late at night.
It sounds like
knock-knock-knockety-knock.
It makes it very hard to sleep."
Corny sighed.
"What happens next?"
Hamster Holmes asked.

"Well, that's the mystery,"
Corny explained.
"When I get out of bed
and open the front door . . .
no one is there!
This has happened
three nights in a row!"

"How strange!"
Hamster Holmes said,
taking a sip from his water bottle.
He was thinking really, really hard.

"Cheer up, Corny,"
Hamster Holmes continued.
"We will come to your house
and look for clues!"
Dr. Watt lit up brightly.
"Thank you both," said Corny.
"See you later!"

After Corny left,
Hamster Holmes and Dr. Watt
hurried off to the park.
Hamster Holmes always did
his best thinking there,
running on the wheel.

After a quick run on the wheel,
he stepped off of it,
tipped back his hat,
and sniffed the air.

"I think I know where to start!"
Hamster Holmes continued.
"We must work this case
from the inside out.
I will stay *inside* Corny's house,
while you stay *outside*.
Let's go solve a mystery!"
Dr. Watt nodded.

When they arrived at
Corny's house,
they looked for clues.

They noticed that
the grass was trimmed,
the windows were clean,
and there wasn't a speck of dirt
to be found.

Hamster Holmes
knocked on the door.
It took Corny a while
to open it.

He had always moved slowly,
but being sleepy made him
really drag his paws—
and his big, bushy tail.

"Come in, come in!" Corny said.
"I was just warming some milk.
It helps me sleep. Will you join
me?"
"We had better not,"
Hamster Holmes replied.
"We need to stay awake tonight."

Then they went to work.
Hamster Holmes stayed inside
to see the mystery from Corny's
point of view.

Dr. Watt went outside.
"He is small enough to
observe in secret,"
Hamster Holmes told Corny.

Only a few minutes had passed
when they heard a *knock, knock.*
Corny jumped.
But it was just a tree branch
hitting the window.

They waited and waited,
but it was quiet.

Then, at last, there was a
knock-knock-knockety-knock.
By the time Hamster Holmes
raced to the door,
no one was there.
"Did you see anything?"
he asked Dr. Watt.

Dr. Watt replied in Morse code, with dots and dashes: *B-I-R-D*. "Did you spell 'bird'? Are you sure?" Hamster Holmes asked. "It's not easy for birds to knock with their wings."

Dr. Watt looked confused.

That is when Hamster Holmes
saw a tiny hole in the door.
"Are you making a peephole?"
he asked.
"No," said Corny,
"What a strange question!"
Then Hamster Holmes saw
sawdust on the doormat.

"If you're not making a peephole,"
said Hamster Holmes,
"then the mystery is . . . solved!"
He turned to Dr. Watt.
"I never should have doubted you.
I know you are a great speller!"

They had just gone inside
when there was another
knock-knock-knockety-knock.
Hamster Holmes opened the door
lickety-split . . .
and a bird flew in!
It wasn't just any bird, either.
It was a woodpecker!

"Just as we suspected!"
Hamster Holmes told Corny.
"This bird knocks with his beak,
causing a hole to form in the door
and dust to fall on the mat.
We didn't see it earlier because
you sweep the floors every day!
But why was he knocking?"

"I'm Russell, your new neighbor,"
said the woodpecker.
"My fridge hasn't arrived yet,
so I was hoping to borrow milk.
It helps me sleep."
"Me too!" said Corny.

The new friends all drank
warm milk together.
"So, now that this mystery
is solved, what's your next case?"
asked Corny.
"I hope it's . . . the Case
of the Oatmeal Cookies,"
said Hamster Holmes.
"I'm hungry!"